MIKE YOUNG

SUPERTED
AND THE GOLD MINES

*Illustrations by Chris Fenna
and Mike Wall*

Muller

Beneath the surface of the earth lie a variety of precious metals. Over the centuries man has dug quarries and sunk mines into the ground in search of copper, iron, and the most valuable metal of all — gold.

In a gold mine somewhere in Africa, a man was at work, drilling into the rockface in a dark tunnel. The drill made so much noise, and he was concentrating so hard on his work, that he did not notice three men step out of the darkness behind him.

These were no ordinary men. They were Texas Pete, Bulk and Skeleton, three of the most evil, and most stupid, villains to ever walk the earth.

Beneath a tree house, many miles away, SuperTed and Spottyman were playing football.

"Don't head it so hard, Spotty!" shouted SuperTed, as the black and white, spotted football ballooned into the air. "If you're not careful, you'll send it into orbit."

"Ha, ha," laughed Spotty. "The Planet Earth could do with a spotty satellite."

They were so busy enjoying themselves, that they did not notice the video screen in the tree house flicker into life. Someone was in danger and needed help!

The ball that Spotty had headed bounced onto the balcony of the tree house and in through the window.

"I'll fetch it, SuperTed," called Spotty, and he started to climb up the tree. As he arrived at the window, he looked in and saw the video screen flicker with life.

"By the bald birds of Spot!" he shouted. "Come here quickly, SuperTed! Someone has been trying to contact us!"

SuperTed was there in a flash, but by the time he had climbed through the window, the picture had disappeared.

"Did you see who it was, Spotty?"

"It was a black man, SuperTed, and there was a large, metal wheel spinning behind him."

"That sounds like a mine shaft, Spotty, but where could it be?"

Deep in the underground tunnel, the miner stopped drilling and brushed the sweat off his forehead. Suddenly he heard a voice behind him.

"Keep your hands loose and turn round real slow!"

The miner spun round, and found himself looking down the barrel of Texas Pete's pistol.

"Get him, Bulk," snarled Tex.

"Anything you say, Tex," said Bulk, and he hurled himself at the startled man. Now the miner was no fool, and as Bulk came towards him, he neatly stepped to one side. Bulk lost his balance and fell onto a conveyor belt, which dropped him into a metal truck loaded with pieces of rock.

The miner may have escaped Bulk, but Texas Pete quickly grabbed him by the collar. "Got you! Now don't try anything funny. All of you, load those trucks with gold!"

Soon the trucks were loaded. Texas Pete tied up the miner and left him by the rockface. Then he climbed on top of the gold and told Skeleton and Bulk to push. The tunnel led uphill and Skeleton was soon very tired.

"Oh, at times like this I wish I had a few muscles."

"Keep pushing, you varmints!" yelled Tex, angrily. "Let's get this gold out of the mine and somewhere safe!"

As they pushed, Bulk's vest caught on a chain which hung from a wooden support.

Creak! Crash! The wood gave way, a crack appeared in the roof of the tunnel, and rocks began to shower down.

"You idiot, Bulk!" shouted Tex. "Quick! Push the truck into the old mine workings!"

By now, SuperTed had said his magic word, Spotty had strapped on his rocket pack, and the two friends were flying over the grasslands of Africa.

"It's no good, SuperTed. We'll never find it," moaned Spotty.

"We've been to tin mines, coal mines, copper mines, and we haven't found a sign of trouble."

As they flew over a small hill, they heard a mournful, wailing sound.

"What's that down there? An alarm! Bubbling blancmange, Spotty, I think this is it!" cried SuperTed, and they flew down to find a small gold mine.

On the ground, the alarm was ringing, and men were rushing back and forth in panic. As soon as SuperTed landed, a mining official dashed towards him.

"SuperTed! You're too late! We've had intruders in the mine . . . and now the roof is collapsing . . . and there is still someone down there!"

Texas Pete, Bulk and Skeleton had found the old mine workings and escaped from the rockfall. Slowly they pushed the truckload of gold through the cramped, dusty tunnel.

"Keep pushing, boys! We're almost there."

"I can't push any more, Tex," grumbled Skeleton. "I'm aching in every bone in my body. Why don't you push?"

"What?" screeched Tex, but before he could explain that he was the boss and Skeleton was there simply to obey orders, Bulk interrupted him.

"Look, Tex. Daylight!"

Meanwhile, SuperTed and Spottyman stepped into a cage which took them down into the bowels of the mine. Once they reached the bottom, they ran quickly through the tunnel. The timbers that held up the roof were creaking with the strain, and loose stones and pebbles showered through cracks in the rock.

"We're just in time!" shouted SuperTed, as he caught sight of the unfortunate miner, who was still tied up near the rockface.

"In time to be buried alive!" replied Spotty, and it looked as if he was right. The roof was about to collapse!

"We'll never make it back to the cage!" said SuperTed. "There *must* be another way out!"

"There is," cried the miner, as they untied him. "Through the old mineworks!"

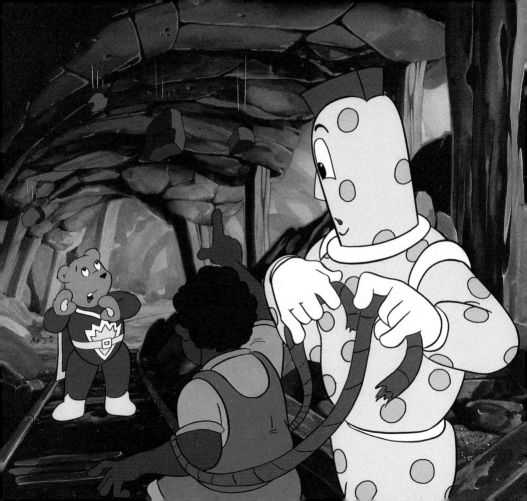

At the same moment the three villains were staggering into the sunlight.

"Ooo Tex," moaned Skeleton, who always liked to have something to complain about. "It's a bit bright. You should have warned me. I would have brought my sunglasses."

Tex paid no attention to him. He had more important things to think about.

"There's only one thing left to do."

"What's that, Tex?" asked Bulk.

"Seal off the mine so nobody can follow us," replied Tex, and he hurled his lasso towards the timbers that held up the entrance to the tunnel. The rope curled round the wooden support and Tex gave it a violent tug, but as the entrance began to collapse, Tex heard the sound of rocket boots. SuperTed had arrived!

SuperTed flew straight towards Tex, knocking him against the truck.

"It's not fair," grumbled Tex. "Billy The Kid never had this trouble with teddy bears."

SuperTed did not stop to listen to him. Rocks were already beginning to block the entrance to the mineworks, and Spotty and the miner were still inside!

With a burst of his rocket boots SuperTed sped towards the falling rocks. Clambering over a boulder he held up the roof with both hands.

"Hurry up, Spotty. I can't hold on much longer," he gasped, but just as the weight became too much for his teddy bear's body to stand, Spotty clambered past, carrying the exhausted miner.

"Thank you, SuperTed. For a moment I thought I would never see the Planet Spot again."

Later, the mining official thanked SuperTed and Spotty for their help. It would take a lot of time to repair the mine, but they had saved the miner's life, and that was far more important than any amount of gold.

As they led the villains away, Spotty turned to SuperTed. "Thank goodness that is over," he said. "Now we can get back to our game of football."

Books in the SuperTed series

SuperTed and the Goldmines
SuperTed and the Pharaoh's Treasure
SuperTed at the Funfair
SuperTed and Nuts in Space
SuperTed Returns to Creepy Castle
SuperTed on Planet Spot
SuperTed and the Train Robbers
SuperTed and the Elephants' Graveyard
SuperTed and the Stolen Rocket Ship
SuperTed and the Pearlfishers
SuperTed and the Inca Treasure
SuperTed and the Giant Kites

SUPERTED is no ordinary bear. He is a teddy bear who can change into SuperTed by whispering a special secret word that only he knows.

Whether at home in his tree house deep in the forest or up in his space-station orbiting Earth, his main mission is to protect children and animals, particularly from the schemes of the evil Texas Pete and his bungling cronies Bulk and Skeleton. SuperTed and his friend Spottyman must try and outwit the terrible trio.

SuperTed stars in an exciting new television series. Now you can follow his adventures in this further series of magic tales.

75p net

ISBN 0-584-62082-9